William Edward Armytage Axon

John Ruskin

A Bibliographical Biography

William Edward Armytage Axon

John Ruskin
A Bibliographical Biography

ISBN/EAN: 9783337010683

Printed in Europe, USA, Canada, Australia, Japan

Cover: Foto ©Raphael Reischuk / pixelio.de

More available books at **www.hansebooks.com**

BIBLIOGRAPHICAL BIOGRAPHY.

1879.

PRICE SIXPENCE.

List of Publications.

Very much above the average of such productions. Many of the papers possess a permanent value, none of them is without interest. . . . We can strongly recommend the volume.— *Westminster Review,* Oct., 1875.

A volume of varied interest.— *British Architect,* July 7, 1876.

It really would be a task to find another volume that tells so much, so happily, that is purchaseable for six shillings.— *Manchester Critic,* August 4, 1876.

A very interesting and instructive volume.— *Preston Chronicle,* Sep. 30, 1876.

The collection contains several good papers, notably those on the circulation of periodicals in Manchester, and on Pepys' system of shorthand.— *Westminster Review,* April, 1877.

JOHN RUSKIN:

A

BIBLIOGRAPHICAL BIOGRAPHY.

By WILLIAM E. A. AXON, M.R.S.L.

[REPRINTED FROM VOL. V. OF THE PAPERS OF THE MANCHESTER LITERARY CLUB.]

1879.

JOHN RUSKIN:

A BIBLIOGRAPHICAL BIOGRAPHY.

BY WILLIAM E. A. AXON, M.R.S.L.

THE literary life of John Ruskin may be said to have extended over half a century. The early dawn of his intellectual powers may be recognized from some childish verses written one month before he had arrived at his ninth year. It was "written on a frosty day, in Glen Farg, just north of Loch Leven," on New Year's Day, 1828 (*Queen of the Air*, p. 128):—

> Papa, how pretty those icicles are,
> That are seen so near, that are seen so far ;
> Those dropping waters that come from the rocks
> And many a hole, like the haunt of a fox.
> That silvery stream that runs babbling along,
> Making a murmuring, dancing song.
> Those trees that stand waving upon the rock's side,
> And men that, like spectres, among them glide.
> And waterfalls that are heard from far,
> And come in sight when very near.
> And the water-wheel that turns slowly round,
> Grinding the corn that—requires to be ground.
> And mountains at a distance seen,
> And rivers winding through the plain.
> And quarries with their craggy stones,
> And the wind among them moans.

The child is father of the man, though the evidences of the parentage are occasionally somewhat difficult to discover. This

boyish rhyme contains, however, no uncertain prophecy. Mr.
Ruskin himself sees in it "all that I ever could be, or all that
I cannot be." Verse-writing was not to be the work of Ruskin's
life; but he did not abandon the muses until about 1850, when
his poems were collected for private circulation. Some of them
had appeared in *Friendship's Offering* and other annuals. From
this very rare volume two pieces may be quoted :—

SONG. (ÆTAT 14.)

I weary for the torrent leaping
　From off the scar's rough crest ;
My muse is on the mountain sleeping,
　My harp is sunk to rest.

I weary for the fountain foaming,
　For shady holm and hill ;
My mind is on the mountain roaming,
　My spirit's voice is still.

I weary for the woodland brook,
　That wanders through the vale ;
I weary for the heights that look
　Adown upon the dale.

The crags are lone on Coniston
　And Loweswater's dell ;
And dreary on the mighty one,
　The cloud enwreathed Scawfell.

Oh ! what although the crags be stern,
　Their mighty peaks that sever,
Fresh flies the breeze on mountain fern,
　And free on mountain heather.

I long to tread the mountain head,
　Above the valley swelling ;
I long to feel the breezes sped
　From grey and gaunt Helvellyn.

I love the eddying circling sweep,
　The mantling and the foam
Of murmuring waters dark and deep
　Amid the valleys lone.

It is a terror, yet 'tis sweet,
　Upon some broken brow
To look upon the distant sweep
　Of ocean spread below.

There is a thrill of strange delight
That passes quivering o'er me,
When blue hills rise upon the sight
Like summer clouds before me.

THE WRECK.

(ÆTAT 19.)

Its masts of might, its sails so free,
Had borne the scatheless keel
Through many a day of darkened sea,
And many a storm of steel ;
When all the winds were calm, it met
(With home-returning prore)
With the lull
Of the waves
On a low lee shore.

The crest of the conqueror
On many a brow was bright ;
The dew of many an exile's eye
Had dimmed the dancing sight ;
And for love and for victory,
One welcome was in store,
In the lull
Of the waves
On a low lee shore.

The voices of the night are mute
Beneath the moon's eclipse ;
The silence of the fitful flute
Is on the dying lips.
The silence of my lonely heart
Is kept for evermore
In the lull
Of the waves
On a low lee shore.

In 1839, Mr. Ruskin gained the Newdigate prize for the English poem at the University of Oxford. It was entitled *Salsette and Elephanta.* The quality of his verses are evident. There is, amidst many evidences of juvenility, a command over the music of language, and a rare power of describing the varying impressions of scenery. The boy, reared amidst the glories of hill and lake, and beneath unsullied skies, became a lover of nature. The imagination is as necessary in science as in poetry. It would perhaps not be far wrong to say that every

great man of science is, if not a singer spoiled, at least a poet
in potentiality. Mr. Ruskin's earliest printed pieces were short
articles in Loudon's *Magazine of Natural History*, and were
written when he was sixteen. It will be best to postpone
the indication of Mr. Ruskin's other writings bearing on the
study of nature, until we have seen how his attention was for
many years diverted from them to other fields.

To this period belongs his delightful Legend of Stiria, a fairy
tale, called *The King of the Golden River*, published in 1851,
with Mr. Richard Doyle's illustrations. This was not written for
publication, but for the entertainment of a child-friend in 1841.

Mr. Ruskin had in a rare measure those powers of observation
and of analysis which make a delight of the observation of
landscape. The "book of nature" was no commonplace phrase
to him, but had a real and an intense meaning. The glory of
cloud and sky, of hill and lake, had a special message for him.
This delight in the beauty of landscape made him an early
admirer of Turner, whose pictures of sea and sky seemed a new
heavenly apocalypse. Mr. Ruskin, himself, tells us that the gift of
taking pleasure in landscape "I assuredly possess in a greater
degree than most men, it having been the ruling passion of my
life, and the reason for the choice of its field of labour." The
genius of Turner, the greatest interpreter the world has ever seen
of the subtle and mystic meaning of the beauty of earth and sky,
was unrecognized, and the artist himself was assailed in a manner
which displayed at once the virulence and the ignorance of the
critics. One of these articles, more foolish and more furious
than usual, drew forth the indignation of Ruskin, who knew it to
be "demonstrable that Turner was right and true, and that his
critics were wrong, false, and base." The projected letter of
defence to the journal grew into a pamphlet, and the pamphlet
in its revised and enlarged form was the first volume of *Modern
Painters*. The title originally selected was *Turner and the
Ancients*, but the limitations thus implied were soon overpassed.
"The title was changed and notes on other living painters added
in the first volume, in deference to the advice of friends; probably
wise, for unless the change had been made the book might never
have been read at all."

Modern Painters was fiercely and somewhat clumsily assailed in

Blackwood for October, 1843. One passage, the critic says, "might have been very excusable in a young curate's sermon during his first year of probation, and might have won for him more nosegays and favours than golden opinions" (p. 486). The critic resorts to the dictionary for the meaning of the word "chrysoprase" (Rev. xxi. 20). This laid him open to Mr. Ruskin's retort :—

We are not insulted with opinions on music from persons ignorant of its notes ; nor with treatises on philology by persons unacquainted with the alphabet ; but here is page after page of criticism, which one may read from end to end, looking for something which the writer knows, and finding nothing. Not his own language, for he has to look in his dictionary, by his own confession, for a word occurring in one of the most important chapters of his Bible ; not the commonest traditions of the schools, for he does not know why Poussin was called "learned ; " not the most simple canons of art, for he prefers Lee to Gainsborough ; not the most ordinary facts of nature, for we find him puzzled by the epithet "silver," as applied to the orange-blossom, evidently never having seen anything silvery about an orange in his life, except a spoon.[*]

The critics were not all blind. One of them writing in the *Gentleman's Magazine* for November, 1843, whilst evidently startled by the novelty of the doctrines advanced, ends thus :—

Such is the purpose of this work ; and the boldness of its design is well supported by the diligence and knowledge, and skilfulness displayed in the execution. The author has laid a solid foundation in the broad and philosophical principles he applies to the art ; while, in the very minute, exact, and delicate criticisms he delivers, he shows a practical and artist-like acquaintance with the details of the subject. If his theory is wrong, if his reasonings are incorrect, and his conclusions not warranted, it must arise from other causes than from unacquaintance with his subject, from indolence in the collections of materials, or unskilfulness in using them ; for, undoubtedly, he has deeply investigated the laws and principles of the art he discusses—he has dwelt on it with a lover's fondness, and studied it with a critic's attention. He is also an eloquent and impressive writer ; he has a command of expression adapted to the varying sentiments he wishes to convey, and can describe the captivating beauties of painting in the brilliant colour of poetic diction.

The first volume of *Modern Painters* appeared in 1843 ; the Second in 1846 ; the Third and Fourth in 1856 ; and the Fifth and last in 1860. A new and final edition of the work was issued in 1873.

[*] *Modern Painters* (Preface to Second Edition).

In *Modern Painters* it is necessary to discriminate between the accidental form which the work assumed and the permanent truths it enforces and explains. The book was "not written either for fame or for money, or for conscience' sake, but of necessity," because injustice was being done and falsehood usurping the place of truth. The cardinal principle of Mr. Ruskin's art criticism may be stated in his own words used in describing *Modern Painters* : "It declares the perfectness and eternal beauty of the Work of God, and tests all work of man by concurrence with or subjection to that." Apart from its value as a statement of the principles of art and of art criticism, *Modern Painters* shows extraordinary insight into nature, and power to reproduce the impressions caused by the ceaseless changes of the glory at once evanescent and eternal of shore, and sea, and sky.

He who walks humbly with Nature will seldom be in danger of losing sight of Art. He will commonly find in all that is truly great of man's works something of their original, for which he will regard them with gratitude, and sometimes follow them with respect. While he who takes Art as his authority may entirely lose sight of all that it interprets, and sink at once into the sin of an idolator and the degradation of a slave.*

Mr. Ruskin has decided not to republish *Modern Painters* as a whole ; but a selection, called Readings, "chosen at her pleasure, by the author's friend, the younger lady of the Thwaite, Coniston," was issued in 1875 and 1876, under the title of *Frondes Agrestes* (*i.e.*, the Foliage of the Fields).

The *Seven Lamps of Architecture* (1849) arose out of memoranda prepared in the composition of one of the sections of the then unpublished third volume of *Modern Painters*. It was an attempt to raise a noble art from degradation. This is manifest even in the definition : "Architecture is the art which so disposes and adorns the edifices raised by man for whatsoever uses, that the sight of them contributes to his mental health, power, and pleasure." The "lamps" are the Spirits of Sacrifice, Truth, Power, Beauty, Life, Memory, and Obedience.

Mr. Ruskin now turned aside for a moment to controversial divinity. The *Notes on the Construction of Sheepfolds* was issued in 1851, and it came to a second edition in the same year.

* Pref. to Second Edition *Modern Painters.*

Mr. Hill Burton says that he had been informed "that this book had a considerable run among the Muirland farmers, whose reception of it was not flattering." The third edition, which the author calls the second, was issued in 1875, and contains in the preface this characteristic confession: "It amazes me to find on re-reading it, that, so late as 1851, I had only got the length of perceiving the schisms between sects of Protestants to be criminal and ridiculous, while I still supposed the schisms between Protestants and Catholics to be virtuous and sublime."

In 1851 appeared a tract on *Pre-Raphaelitism*, which was reprinted in 1862. It records his delight at the appearance of a group of men prepared to accept the advice, given at the close of the first volume of *Modern Painters*, to the young artists of England, that they should "go to nature in all singleness of heart, and walk with her laboriously and trustingly, having no other thought but how best to penetrate her meaning; rejecting nothing, selecting nothing, and scorning nothing." They had been rewarded by scurrilous abuse, and Mr. Ruskin therefore came forward in their defence "to point out the kind of merit which, however deficient in some respects, those works possess beyond the possibility of dispute."

The first volume of *The Stones of Venice* appeared in 1851; the second and third in 1853. As in the *Seven Lamps*, the ethical aspect occupies largely the mind of the author. It is not only a treatise on the archæology and history of Venice, but a sermon on the causes of her downfall and decay. To illustrate this work there was issued a sumptuous atlas folio of *Examples of the Architecture of Venice*.

Giotto and his Works in Padua is an explanatory notice of the wood engravings from paintings of that master issued by the Arundel Society in 1854. It does not profess to be a biography of the artist, though it contains an outline of the artist's life, and, in particular, a subtle and suggestive criticism on the well-known anecdote of his drawing of the O. For the Arundel Society Ruskin has also written a notice of the Cavalli monument, and of Tintoretto's paintings of Christ before Pilate and of Christ bearing the Cross.

In 1853 Mr. Ruskin gave a series of *Lectures on Architecture and Painting*, which were printed in the following year. They are intended to give a popular exposition of the principles of art and their application.

The pamphlet on *The Opening of the Crystal Palace*, considered in some of its relations to the prospects of art, was occasioned by the re-erection of Paxton's palace at Sydenham and some of the extravagant utterances occasioned by it.

Well, it may be replied, we need our bridges, and have pleasure in our palaces; but we do not want Miltons, nor Michael Angelos. Truly, it seems so; for, in the year in which the first Crystal Palace was built, there died among us a man whose name, in after ages, will stand with those of the great of all time. Dying, he bequeathed to the nation the whole mass of his most cherished works; and for these three years, while we have been building this colossal receptacle for casts and copies of the art of other nations, these works of our own greatest painter have been left to decay in a dark room near Cavendish Square, under the custody of an aged servant. This is quite natural. But it is also memorable.

There is another interesting fact connected with the history of the Crystal Palace as it bears on that of the art of Europe, namely, that in the year 1851, when all that glittering roof was built, in order to exhibit the petty arts of our fashionable luxury—the carved bedsteads of Vienna, and glued toys of Switzerland, and gay jewelry of France—in that very year, I say, the greatest pictures of the Venetian masters were rotting at Venice in the rain, for want of roof to cover them, with holes made by cannon shot through their canvas. There is another fact, however, more curious than either of these, which will hereafter be connected with the history of the palace now in building; namely, that at the very period when Europe is congratulated on the invention of a new style of architecture, because fourteen acres of ground have been covered with glass, the greatest examples in existence of true and noble Christian architecture were being resolutely destroyed; and destroyed by the effects of the very interest which was slowly beginning to be excited by them.

Another passage in this now rare tract foreshadows also the striving of his soul under the burden of the social misery :—

If, suddenly, in the midst of the enjoyments of the palate and lightnesses of heart of a London dinner-party, the walls of the chamber were parted, and through their gap, the nearest human beings who were famishing, and in misery, were borne into the midst of the company—feasting and fancy-free— if, pale with sickness, horrible in destitution, broken by despair, body by body, they were laid upon the soft carpet, one beside the chair of every guest, would only the crumbs of the dainties be cast to them—would only a passing glance, a passing thought be vouchsafed to them? Yet the actual facts, the real relations of each Dives and Lazarus, are not altered by the intervention of the house wall between the table and the sick bed—by the few feet of ground (how few !) which are indeed all that separate the merriment from the misery.

The pamphlet ended with an earnest plea for the prevention of the desecration and destruction then in progress under the name of restoration, and which has since done such irretrievable mischief.

From 1855 to 1859 Mr. Ruskin issued *Notes on some of the Principal Pictures Exhibited at the Royal Academy* each year. The series was then discontinued, but resumed for the year 1875 only. The *Notes on the Turner Gallery at Marlborough House* appeared in 1856, and show in a brief and compendious form the views of the greatest of English critics on the greatest of landscape painters. Next year there was a privately-printed Catalogue of Sketches, and two editions of a Catalogue of the Turner Exhibition of 1857–8.

Turner's Drawings of the Harbours of England were engraved by Thomas Lupton, and published in 1856, with an illustrative text, by Mr. Ruskin. This book will always have a deep interest alike for the admirers of Turner and of Ruskin. The introduction contains a noble prose-poem in praise of the sea. In *Frondes Agrestes* he notes that he was rather proud of the short sentence in this book, describing a great breaker against rock : "One moment, a flint cave,—the next, a marble pillar,—the next, a fading cloud" (page 73).

The Elements of Drawing, first published in 1857, came to a second edition in the same year. It is interesting as containing his views on the method of art teaching, which should not begin before the age of twelve or fourteen.

"I do not think it advisable," he says, "to engage a child in any but the most voluntary practice of art. If it has talent for drawing, it will be continually scrawling on what paper it can get ; and should be allowed to scrawl at its own free will, due praise being given for every appearance of care, or truth, in its efforts. It should be allowed to amuse itself with cheap colours almost as soon as it has sense enough to wish for them. If it merely daubs the paper with shapeless stains, the colour-box may be taken away till it knows better ; but as soon as it begins painting red coats on soldiers, striped flags to ships, &c., it should have colours at command ; and without restraining its choice of subject in that imaginative and historical art, of a military tendency, which children delight in (generally quite as valuable, by the way, as any historical art delighted in by their elders), it should be gently led by the parents to try to draw, in such childish fashion as may be, the things it can see and likes—birds, or butterflies, or flowers, or fruits. In later years, the indulgence of using the colour should only be granted as a reward, after it has shown care and progress in its drawings with pencil. A limited number of good and amusing prints should always be within a boy's reach ; in these days of cheap illustration he can hardly possess a volume of nursery tales without good woodcuts in it, and should be encouraged to copy what he likes best of this kind ; but should be firmly restricted to a *few* prints and to a few books."

Mr. Ruskin's latest views on the method of art teaching are given in *The Laws of Fésole*. In 1859 appeared *The Elements of Perspective*. The *Two Paths* are lectures on art, and its application to decoration and manufacture, delivered in 1858-9, and printed in 1859. A new edition appeared in 1878. The subjects of these discourses are the deteriorative power of conventional art over nations, the unity of art, modern manufactures and design, the influence of the imagination in architecture, and the work of iron, in nature, art, and policy. The lectures on the *Political Economy of Art*, originally delivered in Manchester in 1857, and printed in the same year, mark a fresh development of Mr. Ruskin's teachings. In his opinion a large number of our so-called merchants are as ignorant of the nature of money as they are reckless, unjust, and unfortunate in its employment. Mr. Ruskin's views as to the adaptability of Gothic to all the requirements of modern life are set forth in his two letters to Dr. Acland, printed in 1859, in the volume descriptive of the Oxford Museum.

Unto this Last is a volume containing four essays on the first principles of political economy, which originally appeared in the *Cornhill Magazine*. The first edition appeared in 1862, the second in 1877. It is a protest against the "idea that an advantageous code of social action may be determined irrespectively of the influence of social affection." The outcry against them was so great that the editor of the *Cornhill*, "with great discomfort to himself," had to limit their number to four.* For the first time, as he believes, he gives, in plain English, a logical definition of wealth. Subsequent essays in *Fraser's Magazine*, in 1862-3, were stopped by the intervention of the orthodox publisher of that periodical. This more systematic treatment of the economical problem finally appeared in 1872 under the title of *Munera Pulveris*. It contains essays on storekeeping, coinkeeping, commerce, government, and mastership.

* *Munera Pulveris*, p. xxii.

The two greatest living prose writers are undoubtedly Carlyle and Ruskin. They are great by reason of their command of style; they are great by their influence upon the lives and thoughts of the generation amongst whom their lot has been cast. We are too close to see in accurate vision either of these men. We lack the perspective of time. Giants in literature themselves, they have each uttered admonitory counsels on the uses of books, the dangers and delights of the study of literature, and their bearing on the life that now is. In *Sesame and Lilies*, which were originally delivered as lectures at Manchester in 1864, we have Mr. Ruskin's views "about books; and about the way we read them, and could or should read them;" as also on the education of women. On books there are many pregnant sentences, as this one which goes to the root of the matter:—

You might read all the books in the British Museum (if you could live long enough), and remain an utterly "illiterate" uneducated person; but that if you read ten pages of a good book, letter by letter—that is to say with real accuracy—you are for evermore in some measure an educated person.

As an example of real reading, he gives that passage from Milton's *Lycidas* about "the pilot of the Galilean lake," and explains it word by word. He indignantly remarks: "If a man spends lavishly on his library you call him mad—a bibliomaniac. But you never call anyone a horse-maniac, though men ruin themselves every day by their horses, and you do not hear of people ruining themselves by their books." It is to be regretted that neither Ruskin nor Carlyle have given lists of the works which they recommend for students. In this respect Emerson has been more systematic, for he has given a long and remarkable list of the great books of all ages.* We may perhaps consider Mr. Ruskin's *Bibliotheca Pastorum* (1876) as an indication of books that he would advise to be read. The two volumes of that series, so far issued, consist of an English translation of *The Economist of Xenophon*, and of *Rock Honeycomb*, being selections from Sir Philip Sidney's Psalter. Each is fitted with an introduction and explanatory notes. Returning to the contents of *Sesame and Lilies*, in addition to the lecture on King's

---

* There is indeed a list at the end of the *Elements of Drawing*, among things to be studied, but it appears to be special and not general in its aim.

Treasuries (*i.e.*, books, &c.), there is a second, entitled Queen's Gardens, which treats of the education of girls.   There were several editions between 1864 and 1871.   In the last there is added also a Dublin lecture on the *Mystery of Life and its Arts.*

Ethics of the Dust appeared in 1866, and again in 1877.   The subject-matter appears from the sub-title, "ten lectures to little housewives on the elements of crystallization."   The *Crown of Wild Olive* contains three lectures on Work, Traffic, and War.   It was published in 1866, and in 1867 had reached a third edition. He complains :—

> But it has not been without displeased surprise that I have found myself totally unable, as yet, by any repetition, or illustration, to force this plain thought into my readers' heads, that the wealth of nations, as of men, consists in substance, not in ciphers; and that the real good of all work, and of all commerce, depends on the final worth of the thing you make, or get by it."

The title of the book is explained in the preface (p. xxxii. of third edition), as being taken from the heathen belief that to those engaged in the contest of life Jupiter gave a crown:—

> No proud one! no jewelled circlet flaming through heaven above the height of the unmerited throne ; only some few leaves of wild olive, cool to the tired brow, through a few years of peace.   It should have been of gold, they thought ; but Jupiter was poor ; this was the best the god could give them. Seeking a greater than this, they had not known it a mockery.   Not in war, not in wealth, not in tyranny, was there any happiness to be found for them— only in kindly peace, fruitful and free.   The wreath was to be of *wild* olive, mark you : the tree that grows carelessly, tufting the rocks with no vivid bloom, no verdure of branch ; only with soft snow of blossom, and scarcely fulfilled fruit, mixed with grey leaf and thornset stem ; no fastening of diadem for you but with such sharp embroidery !   But this, such as it is, you may win while yet you live; type of grey honour and sweet rest.

A revised edition issued in 1873 contains also a lecture on the future of England, delivered in 1869, and an appendix on the political economy of Prussia.

In the spring of 1867, when the working classes were calling out loudly for a reform in Parliament, Mr. Ruskin entered into a lengthy correspondence with Mr. Thomas Dixon, a working cork-cutter of Sunderland, on many of the questions that were then and now of special moment to the industrial population.   These letters were published in the *Manchester Examiner and Times,*

and were read with keen and vivid interest. They have since
been thrice reprinted. *Time and Tide, by Weare and Tyne*, consists of these twenty-five letters to a working-man of Sunderland
on the laws of work. The burden of the work is that parliamentary influence is useless unless they who possess it have made
up their minds as to what they desire from it, and that having
made up their minds they can do what they want for themselves
without Parliament, and no one can do it for them. This volume
deals with "honesty of work and honesty of exchange." *Fors
Clavigera* may, in a certain measure, be regarded as the continuation of this series.

The Queen of the Air, first issued in 1869, is Mr. Ruskin's
contribution to the new and fascinating field of comparative
mythology. It is a study of the Greek myths of cloud and
storm, both in their natural origin and in their deeper significance.
The Queen of the Air is Athena or Minerva, "having supreme
power both over its blessings of calm and wrath of storm ; and,
spiritually, she is the queen of the breath of man, first of the
bodily breathing, which is life to his blood, and strength to his
arm in battle ; and then of the mental breathing, or inspiration,
which is his moral health and habitual wisdom ; wisdom of con-
duct and of the heart, as opposed to the wisdom of imagination
and the brain ; moral, as distinct from intellectual ; inspired, as
distinct from illuminated." There was a second edition of this
work issued in 1874.

With 1871 Mr. Ruskin began the issue of *Fors Clavigera*.
This consists of letters addressed to the workmen and labourers
of Great Britain, and is in the main a continuation of the exposition commenced in the letters to Mr. Thomas Dixon, of his
views on the organization of labour. They are, however, very
discursive, and contain delightful bits of autobiography, art-
criticism, science, history, and almost everything. Running
through them is a fierce indignation against those social in-
equalities, which are evidenced by the death of one man from
starvation and of another from gluttony. The consideration of
these have led Mr. Ruskin to advocate a form of ordered socialism,
which is to be exemplified in St. George's Guild. These socialist
leanings Mr. Ruskin shares with Plato, with Thomas More, and
probably with the church of the early Christians. Eighty-seven

numbers of *Fors* have appeared, the last of which, called No. 3 of a new series, is dated 1st March, 1878.

Fors, he explains, "is the best part of three good English words, Force, Fortitude, and Fortune." The root of the adjective Claviger being either, as he likes to put it, *clava*, a club ; *clavis*, a key ; or, *clavus*, a nail or a rudder; and *gero* meaning to carry, "Clavigera may mean, therefore, either club-bearer, key-bearer, or nail-bearer. Each of these three possible meanings of *Clavigera* corresponds to one of the three meanings of Fors. Fors, the club-bearer, means the strength of Hercules, or of Deed. Fors, the key-bearer, means the strength of Ulysses, or of Patience. Fors, the nail-bearer, means the strength of Lycurgus, or of Law." (*Fors*, No. ii., pp. 2–3; and cf. iii. 5, and xv. 15.)

As Slade Professor Mr. Ruskin delivered seven *Lectures on Art* before the University of Oxford in Hilary Term, 1870, and they were printed in the same year at the Clarendon Press. After the inaugural discourse the subjects are the relation of art to religion, the relation of art to morals, the relation of art to use, and the more technical subjects of line, light, and colour. To accompany this there was printed a catalogue of examples for study in the university galleries. Mr. Ruskin, again as Slade Professor, in 1870, gave lectures on the elements of sculpture before the University of Oxford, and two years later printed six of them under the title of *Aratra Pentelici*—*i.e.*, the Ploughs of Pentelicus, a mountain in Attica where marble abounded. This contains a great deal also relating to the artistic aspect of numismatics. One of the plates ‑is that never-to-be-forgotten comparison of the Apollo of Syracuse and a self-made man of the present day glorifying his own maker. The seventh lecture on sculpture was issued in 1872 in a separate form, and sets forth the relation between Michael Angelo and Tintoretto. It was printed thus that it might be used at once in reference to the drawings exhibited in the galleries, and with a warning word that its business is to point out "what is to be blamed in Michael Angelo and that it assumes the facts of his power to be generally known." The *Eagle's Nest* is a collection of ten lectures on the relation of natural science to art, which were given before the University of Oxford in Lent Term in 1872, and printed in the same year.

Ariadne Florentina is the title given to six lectures on wood and metal engraving, given before the University of Oxford in Michaelmas Term of 1872. These deal with the relation of engraving to other arts in Florence, to the technics of wood and metal engraving, to design in the German schools of engraving as represented by Dürer and Holbein, and in the Florentine schools by Sandro Botticelli. There is an appendix on the present state of engraving in England. The volume entitled *Val d'Arno* contains ten lectures on the Tuscan art directly antecedent to the Florentine year of victories, given before the University of Oxford in Michaelmas Term, 1873, and printed in the following year. The main subject is the art-work of Niccolo and Giovanni Pisano. All the above-named volumes are illustrated by plates, &c., many of them from Ruskin's originals.

Mr. Ruskin's love of nature is shown under another phase in the lectures on Greek and English birds given before the University of Oxford, and printed in 1873 under the title of *Love's Meinie*. This is the old French *meiny*, a household or retinue of servants. Only two parts have so far appeared. The first deals with the robin, and the second with the swallow. The title appears to have been suggested by the description in the *Romance of the Rose* of the God of Love, whose robe has on it figures of birds, whilst around him fly living birds :—

> But nightingales, a full great rout
> That flien over his head about,
> The leaves felden as they flien
> And he was all with birds wrien,
> With popinjay, with nightingale,
> With chelaundre, and with wodewale,
> With finch, with lark, and with archangel.
> He seemed as he were an angell.
> That down were comen from Heaven clear.

Proserpina began in 1875; the fifth part was issued in 1878. It is still incomplete. It is, as the title-page tells us, a series of "studies of wayside flowers, while the air was yet pure among the Alps, and in the Scotland and England which my father knew." The title is chosen with reference to the lines in *The Winter's Tale*, Act iv., Sc. iii., ll. 116–118. In the introduction he gives advice which few of us will wish to see followed :

"If any scientific man thinks his labours are worth the world's attention, let him, also [like Linnæus], write what he has to say in Latin, finishedly and exquisitely, if it take him a month to do a page. But if—which, unless he be one of the chosen of millions, is assuredly the fact—his lucubrations are only of local and temporary consequence, let him write, as clearly as he can, in his native language."

One purpose of the book is to interpret for the young the Latin or Greek names, altering some of the names because they are "founded on some unclean or debasing association," so that "children who learn botany on the system adopted in this book will know the useful and beautiful names of the plants hitherto given, in all languages; the useless and ugly ones they will not know." Whilst insisting on the learning of the Latin, Mr. Ruskin would also preserve the English names, some of which mirror poetic fancies as beautiful as the flowers. This work is illustrated by some fine specimens of Mr. Ruskin's own artistic powers.

Of *Deucalion* the first part appeared in 1875, the fifth in 1878. It is still incomplete. The object of the book is to present to the public "collected studies of the lapse of waves, and life of stones." In the time of Deucalion, according to the classic story, the deluge came on the earth. Mr. Ruskin's familiarity with the sciences of geology and mineralogy is well known. In the introduction to the present work he says :—

But I think it due to my readers, that they may receive what real good there may be in these studies with franker confidence, to tell them that the first sun-portrait ever taken of the Matterhorn (and as far as I know of any Swiss mountain whatever) was taken by me in the year 1849; that the out-lines (drawn by measurement of angle), given in *Modern Painters*, of the Cervin, and aiguilles of Chamouni, are at this day demonstrable by photo-graphy as the trustworthiest then in existence; that I was the first to point out, in my lecture given in the Royal Institution, the real relation of the vertical cleavages to the stratification in the limestone ranges belonging to the chalk formation in Savoy; and that my analysis of the structure of agates (*Geological Magazine*) remains, even to the present day, the only one which has the slightest claim to accuracy of distinction or completeness of arrangement.

The work contains lectures on the Alps and the Jura, the sym-bolic use of the colours of precious stones in heraldry, and on Yewdale and its streamlets, in addition to some controversial matter respecting glacial theories.

The *Mornings in Florence* came out in 1875, and are intended as a further performance of the "real duty" involved in his Oxford professorship, by giving "simple studies of Christian art for English travellers." The book is in the form of letters "written as I would write to any of my friends who asked me what they ought preferably to study in limited time." The first part deals with Giotto's work at Santa Croce; the second describes his painting of the meeting of Joachim and Anna at the Golden Gate in the church of Sta Maria Novella; the third part, " Before the Soldan," deals with Giotto's pictures of the life of St. Francis of Assisi, and especially of that where that noble Italian stands before "the best of Paynim chivalry to declare the message of the gospel." The fifth part, "The Vaulted Book," describes the "Spanish Chapel" of Sta Maria Novella, which is continued in the next part under the title of the "Strait Gate." The sixth part is "The Shepherd's Tower," and explains the meanings of the bas reliefs in which Giotto has given us his views of the mysteries of life and of religion. The *Mornings in Florence* have been left so far incomplete, the last belonging to the year 1876.

Venice is the subject of some of his smaller works. *St. Mark's Rest* (1877) is described as the History of Venice written for the help of the few travellers who still care for her monuments. It was intended to extend to twelve parts and two supplements. Two parts only have been issued, and one supplement devoted to a description of the pictures by Carpaccio in the chapel of San Giorgio de' Schiavoni. Mr. Ruskin issued in the same year a guide to the principal pictures in the Academy of the Fine Arts at Venice, intended in a similar manner for the use of English travellers.

His views on the teaching of art are further explained and exemplified in *The Laws of Fésole* (1877–8), of which two parts have appeared. The title is derived from the hermit home of Angelico, and the book is "a familiar treatise on the elementary principles and practice of drawing and painting as determined by the Tuscan masters." Mr. Ruskin regards the very name of Schools of Design as involving "the profoundest of Art fallacies. Drawing may be taught by tutors but Design only by Heaven; and to every scholar who thinks to sell his inspiration Heaven refuses its help." The first chapter

is headed by that pregnant sentence, " All great art is praise."
Some of the aphorisms contain instruction put in a humorous
form :—

" Please paint me my white cat," said little Imelda. " Child," answered
the Bolognese Professor, "in the grand school all cats are grey."

Be economical in everything, but especially in candles. When it is time
to light them, go to bed. But the worst wastè of them is drawing by them.

" I can do what I like with my colours, now," said the proud young
scholar. " So could I at your age," answered the master ; "but now, I can
only do what other people like."

The title is thus explained :—

Under the term " Laws of Fésole," therefore, may be most strictly and
accurately arranged every principle of art, practised at its purest source, from
the twelfth to the fifteenth century inclusive. And the purpose of this book
is to teach our English students of art the elements of these Christian laws,
as distinguished from the Infidel laws of the spuriously classic school, under
which, of late, our students have been exclusively trained. Nevertheless, in
this book the art of Giotto and Angelico is not taught because it is Christian,
but because it is absolutely true and good ; neither is the Infidel art of
Palladio and Giulio Romano forbidden because it is Pagan ; but because it is
false and bad ; and has entirely destroyed not only our English schools of art,
but all others in which it has ever been taught, or trusted in.

Fésole, an eminence hard by Florence, is introduced by Milton
in his great epic, with the accent on the last syllable, as one of
the places whence Galileo studied the heavens (Book i., l. 289).

This book is called *The Laws of Fésole* because the entire system of
possible Christian Art is founded on the principles established by Giotto in
Florence, he receiving them from the Attic Greeks through Cimabue, the last
of their disciples, and engrafting them on the existing art of the Etruscans,
the race from which both his master and he were descended.—(Preface,
pp. xii., xiii.)

He therefore ranges under the term every principle of art, practised at its purest source, from the twelfth to the fifteenth century
inclusive. Plate iii. of the *Ariadne Florentina*, page 114, is a
reproduction of Baccïo Bandini's Astrologia, under which is
engraved Milton's line, above referred to :—

At ev'ning, from the top of Fesolè.

In March, 1878, there was an exhibition of the Turner drawings belonging to Mr. Ruskin at the Fine Art Society's galleries.
For this Mr. Ruskin issued a thin volume of explanatory notes.

The epilogue, left incomplete through the writer's illness, contains much interesting matter respecting his early acquisition of Turner's drawings. A very sumptuous edition of these notes, with illus-trations in photogravure, has also appeared. How sadly falls the sound of the words with which Mr. Ruskin closes his preface :—

> Morning breaks as I write, along those Coniston Fells, and the level mists, motionless and grey beneath the rose of the moorlands, veil the lower woods, and the sleeping village, and the long lawns by the lake-shore. Oh, that some one had but told me, in my youth, when all my heart seemed to be set on these colours and clouds, that appear for a little while then vanish away, how little my love of them would serve me, when the silence of lawn and wood, in the dews of morning, should be completed ; and all my thoughts be of those whom, by neither, I was to meet more !

This lengthy list by no means represents the full extent of Mr. Ruskin's literary activity. What have been named are his prin-cipal works, but in addition he has contributed to the *Archi-tectural Magazine*, *Quarterly Review*, the *Contemporary*, the *Nineteenth Century*, and other reviews, to the Transactions of the Royal Institute of British Architects, of the Geological and of the Meteorological Societies. In *Fors* (No. lxxv., Dec., 1875) he states that he had seven books in the press at once— "and any one of them enough to take up the remainder of my life." We have his own testimony that he has also collections for other works. In the preface to *Deucalion* (1875) he says :—

> Of these materials, I have now enough by me for a more interesting (in my own opinion) history of fifteenth-century Florentine art, in six octavo volumes; an analysis of the Attic art of the fifth century B.C., in three volumes ; an exhaustive history of northern thirteenth-century art, in ten volumes; a life of Turner, with analysis of modern landscape art, in four volumes; a life of Walter Scott, with analysis of epic art, in seven volumes ; a life of Xenophon, with analysis of the general principles of Education, in ten volumes ; a com-mentary on Hesiod, with final analysis of the principles of Political Economy, in nine volumes ; and a general description of the geology and botany of the Alps, in twenty-four volumes.

What, then, is the teaching of Ruskin,—taught with so much passion and fervour, with such wealth of illustration, with such power and melody of language. It is that Art should be true to Nature, and that Man should be true to God. When Art loses its faith in Nature, it ceases to possess utility. When Man ceases to work Righteousness, there follow disorders and social perils of every kind. Ruskin beholds in our modern society an aristocracy which has abdicated its functions, a middle class largely given up to greed, a working class struggling in the dark, but dimly conscious of injustice. He sees the fair fields replaced by "jerry-built" houses, the lechery, the drunkenness, the brutality that disgrace our towns and degrade men and women below the level of the beasts, and put them on a par with the fiends of the pit. He says we want Reverence, Obedience, and Organization, to grapple with these evils. He not only denounces the wrong, but has a method for its redress. Even if it prove impracticable, we still owe him a debt of gratitude. He has taught us, perhaps more than any man, the glory of the visible universe. He has taught us also that it is an ill return for God's gift of delight in beauty and order to leave our brethren festering in misery and despair.

NOTE.—The preparation of this paper has been helped by the well stored library and scholarly courtesy of Mr. J. E. Bailey, F.S.A. Free use has also been made of the almost complete series of Mr. Ruskin's works in the Manchester Free Library.

PAPERS. Vol. III. Session 1876-7.
Pp. vi and 308. Price, cloth, Seven Shillings and Sixpence - - - - - - - - - - - - - - 1877.

CONTENTS.

With abstracts of papers by the Rev. R. Henry Gibson, B.A., John Evans,
    William Goldthorpe, Walter Tomlinson, and Charles Madeley ; and an
    Appendix containing Notabilia of the Chetham Library, a List of Lanca-
    shire and Cheshire Publications in 1876, and an Index to the first Three
    Volumes of the Club Papers.

The third volume of the *Papers of the Manchester Literary Club* is fully as interesting
as the preceding volumes ; the number of subjects, copiously or briefly treated, shows in
what various fields of literature, archæology, and art, the members of the club are gathering
or gleaning. There are good examples of nervous style in the book, nor is humour discarded
from its pages. . . . Just now intending tourists are hunting their shelves or persecuting
the booksellers for nice reading "by the sad sea waves," or, on a rainy day, in rural
lodgings ; and, to our thinking, one of the likeliest books to take would be this volume of
the Manchester Literary Club Papers.—*Manchester Critic*, August 24, 1877.

PAPERS. Vol. IV. Session 1877-8.
With Illustrations from original drawings, by R. G.
Somerset, William Meredith, Christopher Blacklock,
Walter Tomlinson, and Elias Bancroft ; portrait of
Butterworth, the mathematician ; and two views of
Clayton Old Hall. Price, cloth, Seven Shillings and
Sixpence - - - - - - - - - - - - - 1878.

CONTENTS :

And other papers by J. H. Nodal, William Lawson, Charles Rowley, jun.,
    Rev. R. H. Gibson, B.A., Charles Hardwick, Abel Heywood, jun.,
    Leonard D. Ardill, Edward Kirk, M. J. Lyons, Edward Williams,
    William Hindshaw, Alfred Owen Legge, and R. J. Udall.

A GLOSSARY of the LANCASHIRE DIALECT. By J. H. Nodal and George Milner. With Etymological Notes and Illustrative Passages from Anglo-Saxon and Middle English Authors and from writers in the Dialect. Part I. containing words from A to E. Price Three Shillings and Sixpence ; Large Paper, Seven Shillings and Sixpence - - - - - - - - - - - - 1875.

A very important and valuable work. . . A most important contribution to philological literature.—*Scotsman*, March 31, 1876.

Not merely a collection of words, but illustrations of them placed in chronological order, ranging from Old English down to the present day. The work thus becomes not merely a scientific history of the English language, but throws the greatest light upon many passages of our older authors.—*Westminster Review*, April, 1876.

It is carefully executed, and may take its place beside the well-known glossaries of Atkinson, Forby, Miss Baker, Barnes, and the rest. . . . The most valuable part lies in the illustrations from books written in the dialect and from colloquial usage.—*Academy*, July 1, 1876.

BIBLIOGRAPHY of LANCASHIRE and CHESHIRE. The publications of the two Counties during 1876. Pp. vii and 38. Price One Shilling - - - - - 1877.

This important record. Nothing so suggestive and so really useful to the general book-trade as this *Bibliography of Lancashire and Cheshire* has hitherto been published in the provinces.—*Bookseller*, September, 1877.

LANCASHIRE AUTHORS. A List, with Brief Biographical and Bibliographical Notes. Edited by Charles William Sutton. Pp. viii and 164. Price Ten Shillings, cloth - - - - - - - - - - - - - - 1876.

The rigid accuracy which has been attempted will be very serviceable. We congratulate Mr. Sutton on the successful issue of his enterprise.—*Manchester Guardian*, Jan. 15, 1877.

This excellent manual. It will save the librarian and the student an incalculable amount of research among out-of-the-way and little known authorities and documents, to say nothing of the fresh information, chiefly about living writers, which is here published for the first time. We congratulate Mr. Sutton and his colleagues of the Manchester Literary Club upon the successful and thoroughly-satisfactory accomplishment of an arduous undertaking. *Manchester City News.*

Publishers to the Manchester Literary Club :

ABEL HEYWOOD & SON, Oldham Street, Manchester ;

AND Catherine Street, Strand, London.

A. Ireland and Co., Printers, Pall Mall, Manchester.

JOHN RUSKIN:

A

BIBLIOGRAPHICAL BIOGRAPHY.

By WILLIAM E. A. AXON, M.R.S.L.

Second Edition.

MANCHESTER : ABEL HEYWOOD AND SON, 56 & 58, OLDHAM-ST.
EDINBURGH : ADAM SMAIL, 19, NORTH BRUNTSFIELD PLACE.
SHEFFIELD : THOMAS ROGERS, CHANGE ALLEY CORNER.

THE RUSKIN SOCIETY, OLD TOWN HALL, MANCHESTER.
1881.

JOHN RUSKIN:

A

BIBLIOGRAPHICAL BIOGRAPHY.

By WILLIAM E. A. AXON, M.R.S.L.

Second Edition.

MANCHESTER: ABEL HEYWOOD AND SON, 56 & 58, OLDHAM-ST.
EDINBURGH: ADAM SMAIL, 19, NORTH BRUNTSFIELD PLACE.
SHEFFIELD: THOMAS ROGERS, CHANGE ALLEY CORNER.
THE RUSKIN SOCIETY, OLD TOWN HALL, MANCHESTER.
1881.

THE rapid sale of the first edition of this pamphlet appears to show that it supplied a public need. It has been for some time out of print, and is now reissued, with corrections and additions. Soon after the formation of the Ruskin Society, a visit was paid to the Manchester Free Library, and, in response to a request then made, an extemporaneous address was given on the collection of Mr. Ruskin's works to be found in that institution. That address forms the basis of the present brief introduction to his writings. Mr. R. H. Shepherd's excellent "Bibliography of Ruskin" has other aims, and goes into details which would be out of place here. Free use has been made of the Ruskin collection in the Manchester Free Library, which is believed to be the completest in any public library. The preparation of the paper has also been helped by the well-stored library and scholarly courtesy of Mr. J. E. Bailey, F.S.A. To Mr. W. A. Turner thanks are gratefully returned for the loan of some precious volumes.

FERN BANK, HIGHER BROUGHTON,
MANCHESTER, AUG., 1881.

** Mr. Ruskin's publisher is Mr. George Allen, Sunnyside, Orpington, Kent.

JOHN RUSKIN:

A BIBLIOGRAPHICAL BIOGRAPHY.

THE literary life of John Ruskin may be said to have extended over half a century. The early dawn of his intellectual powers may be recognized from some childish verses written one month before he had arrived at his ninth year. They were "written on a frosty day, in Glen Farg, just north of Loch Leven," on New Year's Day, 1828 (*Queen of the Air*, p. 128):—

> Papa, how pretty those icicles are,
> That are seen so near, that are seen so far ;
> Those dropping waters that come from the rocks
> And many a hole, like the haunt of a fox.
> That silvery stream that runs babbling along,
> Making a murmuring, dancing song.
> Those trees that stand waving upon the rock's side,
> And men that, like spectres, among them glide.
> And waterfalls that are heard from far,
> And come in sight when very near.
> And the water-wheel that turns slowly round,
> Grinding the corn that—requires to be ground.
> And mountains at a distance seen,
> And rivers winding through the plain.
> And quarries with their craggy stones,
> And the wind among them moans.

The child is father of the man, though the evidences of the parentage are occasionally somewhat difficult to discover. The boyish rhyme contains, however, no uncertain prophecy. Mr. Ruskin himself sees in it "all that I ever could be, or all that I cannot be." Verse-writing was not to be the work of Ruskin's life ; but he did not abandon the muses until about 1850, when

his poems, some of which had appeared in *Friendship's Offering*
and other annuals, were collected for private circulation.   From
this very rare volume two pieces may be quoted :—

SONG. (ÆTAT 14.)

I weary for the torrent leaping
   From off the scar's rough crest ;
My muse is on the mountain sleeping,
   My harp is sunk to rest.

I weary for the fountain foaming,
   For shady holm and hill ;
My mind is on the mountain roaming,
   My spirit's voice is still.

I weary for the woodland brook,
   That wanders through the vale ;
I weary for the heights that look
   Adown upon the dale.

The crags are lone on Coniston
   And Loweswater's dell ;
And dreary on the mighty one,
   The cloud enwreathed Scawfell.

Oh ! what although the crags be stern,
   Their mighty peaks that sever,
Fresh flies the breeze on mountain fern,
   And free on mountain heather.

I long to tread the mountain head,
   Above the valley swelling ;
I long to feel the breezes sped
   From grey and gaunt Helvellyn.

I love the eddying circling sweep,
   The mantling and the foam
Of murmuring waters dark and deep
   Amid the valleys lone.

It is a terror, yet 'tis sweet,
   Upon some broken brow
To look upon the distant sweep
   Of ocean spread below.

There is a thrill of strange delight
That passes quivering o'er me,
When blue hills rise upon the sight
Like summer clouds before me.

THE WRECK.

(ÆTAT 19.)

Its masts of might, its sails so free,
Had borne the scatheless keel
Through many a day of darkened sea,
And many a storm of steel ;
When all the winds were calm, it met
(With home-returning prore)
With the lull
Of the waves
On a low lee shore.

The crest of the conqueror
On many a brow was bright ;
The dew of many an exile's eye
Had dimmed the dancing sight ;
And for love and for victory,
One welcome was in store,
In the lull
Of the waves
On a low lee shore.

The voices of the night are mute
Beneath the moon's eclipse ;
The silence of the fitful flute
Is on the dying lips.
The silence of my lonely heart
Is kept for evermore
In the lull
Of the waves
On a low lee shore.

In 1839, Mr. Ruskin gained the Newdigate prize for the English poem at the University of Oxford. It was entitled *Salsette and Elephanta*, and was reprinted in 1879. The quality of his verses is evident. There is, amidst many evidences of juvenility, a command over the music of language, and also a rare power of describing the varying impressions of scenery. The boy became

an ardent lover of nature. The imagination is as necessary in
science as in poetry. It would perhaps not be far wrong to say
that every great man of science is, if not a singer spoiled, at least
a poet in potentiality. Mr. Ruskin's earliest printed pieces were
short articles in Loudon's *Magazine of Natural History* and were
written when he was sixteen. He contributed some articles on
Art and Architecture to the *Architectural Magazine* in 1837.*

To this period belongs his delightful Legend of Stiria, a fairy
tale, called *The King of the Golden River*, published in 1851, with
Mr. Richard Doyle's illustrations. This was not written for publication, but for the entertainment of a child-friend in 1841.

Mr. Ruskin had in a rare measure those powers of observation
and of analysis which make a delight of the observation of
landscape. The "book of nature" was no commonplace phrase
to him, but had a real and an intense meaning. The glory of
cloud and sky, of hill and lake, had a special message for him.
This delight in the beauty of landscape made him an early
admirer of Turner, whose pictures of sea and sky seemed a new
heavenly apocalypse. Mr. Ruskin himself tells us that the gift of
taking pleasure in landscape "I assuredly possess in a greater
degree than most men, it having been the ruling passion of my
life, and the reason for the choice of its field of labour." The
genius of Turner, the greatest interpreter the world has ever seen
of the subtle and mystic meaning of the beauty of earth and sky,
was unrecognized, and the artist himself was assailed in a manner

---

* These papers have not been republished in England, but there is an
American edition, entitled, *The Poetry of Architecture, to which is added
Suggestions on Works of Art, by Kata Phusin, conjectured nom de plume of
John Ruskin.* (New York : John Wiley and Son, 1873.) The same publishers have issued a uniform edition of the more important of Mr. Ruskin's
works—whether with or without leave might be too curious an inquiry. They
have also issued the following : *Precious Thoughts, Moral and Religious,
gathered from the works of John Ruskin, by Mrs. L. C. Tuthill.* (New York :
1879.) *The True and the Beautiful in Nature, Art, Morals, and Religion,
selected from the works of John Ruskin, with a Notice of the Author, by Mrs.
L. C. Tuthill.* New York : 1873.) *Art Culture : A Handbook of Art
Technicalities and Criticisms, selected from the works of John Ruskin, and
arranged and supplemented by Rev. W. H. Platt.* (New York : 1873.) Here
we may name the now rare volume of *Selections from the Writings of John
Ruskin.* (London : Smith, Elder, and Co. 1871.)

which displayed at once the virulence and the ignorance of the critics. One of these articles, more foolish and more furious than usual, drew forth the indignation of Ruskin, who knew it to be " demonstrable that Turner was right and true, and that his critics were wrong, false, and base." The projected letter of defence to the journal grew into a pamphlet, and the pamphlet in its revised and enlarged form was the first volume of *Modern Painters*. The title originally selected was *Turner and the Ancients*, but the limitations thus implied were soon overpassed. "The title was changed, and notes on other living painters added in the first volume, in deference to the advice of friends; probably wise, for unless the change had been made the book might never have been read at all."

Modern Painters was fiercely and somewhat clumsily assailed in *Blackwood* for October, 1843. One passage, the critic says, "might have been very excusable in a young curate's sermon during his first year of probation, and might have won for him more nosegays and favours than golden opinions" (p. 486). The critic resorts to the dictionary for the meaning of the word "chrysoprase" (Rev. xxi. 20). This laid him open to Mr. Ruskin's retort :—

We are not insulted with opinions on music from persons ignorant of its notes; nor with treatises on philology by persons unacquainted with the alphabet; but here is page after page of criticism, which one may read from end to end, looking for something which the writer knows, and finding nothing. Not his own language, for he has to look in his dictionary, by his own confession, for a word occurring in one of the most important chapters of his Bible; not the commonest traditions of the schools, for he does not know why Poussin was called " learned;" not the most simple canons of art, for he prefers Lee to Gainsborough; not the most ordinary facts of nature, for we find him puzzled by the epithet " silver," as applied to the orange-blossom, evidently never having seen anything silvery about an orange in his life, except a spoon.*

The critics were not all blind. One of them writing in the *Gentleman's Magazine* for November, 1843, whilst evidently startled by the novelty of the doctrines advanced, ends thus :—

Such is the purpose of this work; and the boldness of its design is well supported by the diligence and knowledge, and skilfulness displayed in the

---

* *Modern Painters* (Preface to Second Edition).

execution. The author has laid a solid foundation in the broad and philosophical principles he applies to the art ; while, in the very minute, exact, and
delicate criticisms he delivers, he shows a practical and artist-like acquaintance
with the details of the subject. If his theory is wrong, if his reasonings are
incorrect, and his conclusions not warranted, it must arise from other causes
than from unacquaintance with his subject, from indolence in the collections
of materials, or unskilfulness in using them ; for, undoubtedly, he has deeply
investigated the laws and principles of the art he discusses—he has dwelt on
it with a lover's fondness, and studied it with a critic's attention. He is also
an eloquent and impressive writer ; he has a command of expression adapted
to the varying sentiments he wishes to convey, and can describe the captivating
beauties of painting in the brilliant colour of poetic diction.

The first volume of *Modern Painters* appeared in 1843 ; the
Second in 1846 ; the Third and Fourth in 1856 ; and the Fifth
and last in 1860. A new and final edition of the work was
issued in 1873.

In *Modern Painters* it is necessary to discriminate between the
accidental form which the work assumed and the permanent
truths it enforces and explains. The book was "not written
either for fame or for money, or for conscience' sake, but of
necessity," because injustice was being done and falsehood
usurping the place of truth. The cardinal principle of Mr.
Ruskin's art criticism may be stated in his own words used in
describing *Modern Painters :* "It declares the perfectness and
eternal beauty of the Work of God, and tests all work of man
by concurrence with or subjection to that." Apart from its
value as a statement of the principles of art and of art criticism,
Modern Painters shows extraordinary insight into nature, and
power to reproduce the impressions caused by the ceaseless
changes of the glory at once evanescent and eternal of shore,
and sea, and sky.

He who walks humbly with Nature will seldom be in danger of losing
sight of Art. He will commonly find in all that is truly great of man's works
something of their original, for which he will regard them with gratitude, and
sometimes follow them with respect. While he who takes Art as his authority
may entirely lose sight of all that it interprets, and sink at once into the sin
of an idolator and the degradation of a slave.*

Mr. Ruskin has decided not to republish *Modern Painters* as a

---

* Pref. to Second Edition *Modern Painters.*

whole; but a selection, called Readings, "chosen at her pleasure, by the author's friend, the younger lady of the Thwaite, Coniston," was issued in 1875 and 1876, under the title of *Frondes Agrestes* (*i.e.*, the Foliage of the Fields).

The *Seven Lamps of Architecture* (1849) arose out of memoranda prepared in the composition of one of the sections of the then unpublished third volume of *Modern Painters*. It was an attempt to raise a noble art from degradation. This is manifest even in the definition: "Architecture is the art which so disposes and adorns the edifices raised by man for whatsoever uses, that the sight of them contributes to his mental health, power, and pleasure." The "lamps" are the Spirits of Sacrifice, Truth, Power, Beauty, Life, Memory, and Obedience. A second edition appeared in 1880. In the preface Mr. Ruskin says: "I never intended to have republished this book, which has become the most useless I ever wrote; the buildings it describes with so much delight being now either knocked down or scraped and patched into smugness and smoothness more tragic than uttermost ruin."

Mr. Ruskin now turned aside for a moment to controversial divinity. The *Notes on the Construction of Sheepfolds* was issued in 1851, and it came to a second edition in the same year. Mr. Hill Burton says that he had been informed "that this book had a considerable run among the Muirland farmers, whose reception of it was not flattering." The third edition, which the author calls the second, was issued in 1875, and contains in the preface this characteristic confession: "It amazes me to find on re-reading it, that, so late as 1851, I had only got the length of perceiving the schisms between sects of Protestants to be criminal and ridiculous, while I still supposed the schisms between Protestants and Catholics to be virtuous and sublime."

In 1851 appeared a tract on *Pre-Raphaelitism*, which was reprinted in 1862. It records his delight at the appearance of a group of men prepared to accept the advice, given at the close of the first volume of *Modern Painters*, to the young artists of England, that they should "go to nature in all singleness of heart, and walk with her laboriously and trustingly, having no other thought but how best to penetrate her meaning; rejecting nothing, selecting nothing, and scorning nothing." They had been rewarded by scurrilous abuse, and Mr. Ruskin therefore came forward in their defence "to point out the kind of merit which, however deficient in some respects, those works possess beyond the possibility of dispute."

The first volume of *The Stones of Venice* appeared in 1851; the second and third in 1853. As in the *Seven Lamps*, the ethical aspect occupies largely the mind of the author. It is not only a treatise on the archæology and history of Venice, but a sermon on the causes of her downfall and decay.* To illustrate this work there was issued a sumptuous atlas folio of *Examples of the Architecture of Venice.*

Giotto and his Works in Padua is an explanatory notice of the wood engravings from paintings of that master issued by the Arundel Society in 1854. It does not profess to be a biography of the artist, though it contains an outline of the artist's life, and, in particular, a subtle and suggestive criticism on the well-known anecdote of his drawing of the O. For the Arundel Society Ruskin has also written a notice of the Cavalli monument, and of Tintoretto's paintings of Christ before Pilate and of Christ bearing the Cross.

In 1853 Mr. Ruskin gave a series of *Lectures on Architecture and Painting*, which were printed in the following year. They are intended to give a popular exposition of the principles of art and their application. A second edition appeared in 1855.

The pamphlet on *The Opening of the Crystal Palace Considered in some of its Relations to the Prospects of Art* appeared in 1854, and was occasioned by the re-erection of Paxton's palace at Sydenham and by some of the extravagant utterances it occasioned.

Well, it may be replied, we need our bridges, and have pleasure in our palaces; but we do not want Miltons, nor Michael Angelos. Truly, it seems so; for, in the year in which the first Crystal Palace was built, there died among us a man whose name, in after ages, will stand with those of the great of all time. Dying, he bequeathed to the nation the whole mass of his most cherished works; and for these three years, while we have been building this colossal receptacle for casts and copies of the art of other nations, these works

---

* In 1879 appeared the first vol. of *The Stones of Venice: introductory chapters and local indices, printed separately, for the use of travellers while staying in Venice and Verona.*

of our own greatest painter have been left to decay in a dark room near Cavendish Square, under the custody of an aged servant. This is quite natural. But it is also memorable.

There is another interesting fact connected with the history of the Crystal Palace as it bears on that of the art of Europe, namely, that in the year 1851, when all that glittering roof was built, in order to exhibit the petty arts of our fashionable luxury—the carved bedsteads of Vienna, and glued toys of Switzerland, and gay jewelry of France—in that very year, I say, the greatest pictures of the Venetian masters were rotting at Venice in the rain, for want of roof to cover them, with holes made by cannon shot through their canvas. There is another fact, however, more curious than either of these, which will hereafter be connected with the history of the palace now in building; namely, that at the very period when Europe is congratulated on the invention of a new style of architecture, because fourteen acres of ground have been covered with glass, the greatest examples in existence of true and noble Christian architecture were being resolutely destroyed; and destroyed by the effects of the very interest which was slowly beginning to be excited by them.

Another passage in this now rare tract foreshadows also the striving of his soul under the burden of the social misery :—

If, suddenly, in the midst of the enjoyments of the palate and lightnesses of heart of a London dinner-party, the walls of the chamber were parted, and through their gap, the nearest human beings who were famishing, and in misery, were borne into the midst of the company—feasting and fancy-free— if, pale with sickness, horrible in destitution, broken by despair, body by body, they were laid upon the soft carpet, one beside the chair of every guest, would only the crumbs of the dainties be cast to them—would only a passing glance, a passing thought be vouchsafed to them? Yet the actual facts, the real relations of each Dives and Lazarus, are not altered by the intervention of the house wall between the table and the sick bed—by the few feet of ground (how few !) which are indeed all that separate the merriment from the misery.

The pamphlet ended with an earnest plea for the prevention of the desecration and destruction then in progress under the name of restoration, and which has since done such irretrievable mischief.

From 1855 to 1859 Mr. Ruskin issued *Notes on some of the Principal Pictures Exhibited at the Royal Academy* each year.*

---

* In 1876 there was reprinted, for private circulation only, *Letters to the Times on the Principal Pre-Raphaelite Pictures in the Exhibition of 1854.* This tract deals with Hunt's "Light of the World," and "Awakened Conscience."

The series was then discontinued, but resumed for the year 1875 only. The *Notes on the Turner Gallery at Marlborough House* appeared in 1857, and show in a brief and compendious form the views of the greatest of English critics on the greatest of landscape painters. Next year there was a privately-printed *Catalogue of the Turner Sketches* in the National Gallery, and two editions of a *Catalogue of the Sketches and Drawings of W. M. Turner* exhibited at Marlborough House in the year 1857-8.

Turner's drawings of the *Harbours of England* were engraved by Thomas Lupton, and published in 1856, with an illustrative text, by Mr. Ruskin. This book will always have a deep interest alike for the admirers of Turner and of Ruskin. The introduction contains a noble prose-poem in praise of the sea. In *Frondes Agrestes* he notes that he was rather proud of the short sentence in this book, describing a great breaker against rock : " One moment, a flint cave,—the next, a marble pillar,—the next, a fading cloud " (page 73).

The Elements of Drawing, first published in 1857, came to a second edition in the same year. It is interesting as containing his views on the method of art teaching, which should not begin, he considers, before the age of twelve or fourteen.

" I do not think it advisable," he says, " to engage a child in any but the most voluntary practice of art. If it has talent for drawing, it will be continually scrawling on what paper it can get ; and should be allowed to scrawl at its own free will, due praise being given for every appearance of care, or truth, in its efforts. It should be allowed to amuse itself with cheap colours almost as soon as it has sense enough to wish for them. If it merely daubs the paper with shapeless stains, the colour-box may be taken away till it knows better ; but as soon as it begins painting red coats on soldiers, striped flags to ships, &c., it should have colours at command ; and without restraining its choice of subject in that imaginative and historical art, of a military tendency, which children delight in (generally quite as valuable, by the way, as any historical art delighted in by their elders), it should be gently led by the parents to try to draw, in such childish fashion as may be, the things it can see and likes—birds, or butterflies, or flowers, or fruits. In later years, the indulgence of using the colour should only be granted as a reward, after it has shown care and progress in its drawings with pencil. A limited number of good and amusing prints should always be within a boy's reach ; in these day's of cheap illustration he can hardly possess a volume of nursery tales without good woodcuts in it, and should be encouraged to copy what he likes best of this kind ; but should be firmly restricted to a *few* prints and to a few books."

Mr. Ruskin's latest views on the method of art teaching are given in *The Laws of Fésole*. The inaugural address, delivered at the Cambridge School of Art, October 29th, 1858, was printed, and a second edition appeared in 1879. The address concludes with these impressive words :—

> He only can be said to be educated in Art to whom all his work is only a feeble sign of glories which he cannot convey, and a feeble means of measuring, with ever enlarging admiration, the great and intraversable gulf which God has set between the great and the common intelligence of mankind ; and all the triumphs of Art which man can commonly achieve are only truly crowned by pure delight in natural scenes themselves, and by the sacred and self-forgetful veneration which can be nobly abashed, and tremblingly exalted, in the presence of a human spirit greater than his own.

In 1859 appeared *The Elements of Perspective*. The *Two Paths* are lectures on art and its application to decoration and manufacture, delivered in 1858-9, and printed in 1859. " The law which it has been my effort chiefly to illustrate is the dependence of all noble design in any kind on the sculpture or painting of Organic Form" (Preface). A new edition appeared in 1878. The subjects of these discourses are the deteriorative power of conventional art over nations, the unity of art, modern manufactures and design, the influence of the imagination in architecture, and the work of iron, in nature, art, and policy. The lectures on the *Political Economy of Art*, originally delivered in Manchester in 1857, and printed in the same year, mark a fresh development of Mr. Ruskin's teachings. In his opinion a large number of our so-called merchants are as ignorant of the nature of money as they are reckless, unjust, and unfortunate in its employment. Mr. Ruskin's views as to the adaptability of Gothic to all the requirements of modern life are set forth in his two letters to Dr. Acland, printed in 1859, in the volume descriptive of the Oxford Museum.

Unto this Last is a volume containing four essays on the first principles of political economy, which originally appeared in the *Cornhill Magazine*. The first edition appeared in 1862, the second in 1877. It is a protest against the "idea that an advantageous code of social action may be determined irrespectively of the influence of social affection." In the second edition there is an additional note added to the preface (p. xiv), which the reader will do well to note. The outcry against them was so great that the editor of the *Cornhill*, " with great discomfort to himself," had to limit their number to four.* For the first time, as he believes, he gives, in plain English, a logical definition of wealth. Subsequent essays in *Fraser's Magazine*, in 1862-3, were stopped by the intervention of the orthodox publisher of that periodical. This more systematic treatment of the economical problem finally appeared in 1872 under the title of *Munera Pulveris*. The book so named contains essays on storekeeping, coinkeeping, commerce, government, and mastership.

The two greatest English prose writers of our day are Carlyle and Ruskin. They are great by reason of their command of style; they are great by their influence upon the lives and thoughts of the generation amongst whom their lot has been cast. We are too close to see in accurate vision either of these men. We lack the perspective of time. Giants in literature themselves, they have each uttered admonitory counsels on the uses of books, the dangers and delights of the study of literature, and their bearing on the life that now is. In *Sesame and Lilies*, which were originally delivered as lectures at Manchester in 1864, we have Mr. Ruskin's views "about books; and about the way we read them, and could or should read them;" as also on the education of women. On books there are many pregnant sentences, as this one which goes to the root of the matter :—

> You might read all the books in the British Museum (if you could live long enough), and remain an utterly "illiterate" uneducated person; but that if you read ten pages of a good book, letter by letter—that is to say with real accuracy—you are for evermore in some measure an educated person.

As an example of real reading, he gives that passage from Milton's *Lycidas* about " the pilot of the Galilean lake," and explains it word by word. He indignantly remarks : " If a man spends lavishly on his library you call him mad—a bibliomaniac. But you never call anyone a horse-maniac, though men ruin themselves every day by their horses, and you do not hear of people ruining themselves by their books." It is to be regretted that neither Ruskin nor Carlyle have given lists of the works which they recommend for students. In this respect Emerson has been

---

more systematic, for he has given a long and remarkable list of the great books of all ages.* We may perhaps consider Mr. Ruskin's *Bibliotheca Pastorum* (1876) as an indication of books that he would advise to be read. Returning to the contents of *Sesame and Lilies*, in addition to the lecture on King's Treasuries (*i.e.*, books, &c.), there is a second, entitled Queen's Gardens, which treats of the education of girls. There were several editions between 1864 and 1871. To the last there is added also a Dublin lecture on the *Mystery of Life and its Arts*.

Ethics of the Dust appeared in 1866, and again in 1877. The subject-matter appears from the sub-title, "ten lectures to little housewives on the elements of crystallization." The *Crown of Wild Olive* contains three lectures on Work, Traffic, and War. It was published in 1866, and in 1867 had reached a third edition. He complains :—

> But it has not been without displeased surprise that I have found myself totally unable, as yet, by any repetition, or illustration, to force this plain thought into my readers' heads, that the wealth of nations, as of men, consists in substance, not in ciphers ; and that the real good of all work, and of all commerce, depends on the final worth of the thing you make, or get by it.

The title of the book is explained in the preface (p. xxxii of third edition), as being taken from the heathen belief that to those engaged in the contest of life Jupiter gave a crown :—

> No proud one ! no jewelled circlet flaming through heaven above the height of the unmerited throne ; only some few leaves of wild olive, cool to the tired brow, through a few years of peace. It should have been of gold, they thought ; but Jupiter was poor ; this was the best the god could give them. Seeking a greater than this, they had not known it a mockery. Not in war, not in wealth, not in tyranny, was there any happiness to be found for them— only in kindly peace, fruitful and free. The wreath was to be of *wild* olive, mark you : the tree that grows carelessly, tufting the rocks with no vivid bloom, no verdure of branch ; only with soft snow of blossom, and scarcely fulfilled fruit, mixed with grey leaf and thornset stem ; no fastening of diadem for you but with such sharp embroidery ! But this, such as it is, you may win while yet you live ; type of grey honour and sweet rest.

---

* There is indeed a list at the end of the *Elements of Drawing*, among things to be studied, but it appears to be special and not general in its aim.

A revised edition issued in 1873 contains also a lecture on the future of England, delivered in 1869, and an appendix on the political economy of Prussia.

In the spring of 1867, when the working classes were calling out loudly for a reform in Parliament, Mr. Ruskin entered into a lengthy correspondence with Mr. Thomas Dixon, a working cork-cutter of Sunderland, on many of the questions that were then and now of special moment to the industrial population. These letters were published in the *Manchester Examiner and Times*, and were read with keen and vivid interest. They have since been thrice reprinted, the last issue being in 1872. *Time and Tide, by Weare and Tyne*, consists of these twenty-five letters to a working-man of Sunderland on the laws of work. The burden of the work is that parliamentary influence is useless unless they who possess it have made up their minds as to what they desire from it, and that having made up their minds they can do what they want for themselves without Parliament, and no one can do it for them. This volume deals with "honesty of work and honesty of exchange." *Fors Clavigera* may, in a certain measure, be regarded as the continuation of this series. In 1868 he con-tributed a preface to the reissue of *Grimm's German Popular Stories*, as translated by Edgar Taylor and illustrated by George Cruikshank. . There have been several subsequent editions.

The Queen of the Air, first issued in 1869, is Mr. Ruskin's contribution to the new and fascinating field of comparative mythology. It is a study of the Greek myths of cloud and storm, both in their natural origin and in their deeper significance. The Queen of the Air is Athena or Minerva, " having supreme power both over its blessings of calm and wrath of storm ; and, spiritually, she is the queen of the breath of man, first of the bodily breathing, which is life to his blood, and strength to his arm in battle ; and then of the mental breathing, or inspiration, which is his moral health and habitual wisdom ; wisdom of con-duct and of the heart, as opposed to the wisdom of imagination and the brain ; moral, as distinct from intellectual ; inspired, as distinct from illuminated." There was a second edition of this work issued in 1874.

With 1871 Mr. Ruskin began the issue of *Fors Clavigera*. This work consists of letters addressed to the workmen and labourers

of Great Britain, and is in the main a continuation of the exposition commenced in the letters to Mr. Thomas Dixon, of his
views on the organization of labour. They are, however, very
discursive, and contain delightful bits of autobiography, art-
criticism, science, history, and almost everything. Running
through them is a fierce indignation against those social in-
equalities, which are evidenced by the death of one man from
starvation and of another from gluttony. The consideration of
these have led Mr. Ruskin to advocate a form of ordered socialism,
which is to be exemplified in St. George's Guild. These socialist
leanings Mr. Ruskin shares with Plato, with Thomas More, and
probably with the church of the early Christians. The eighty-
seventh number of *Fors* (No. 3 of a new series) is dated 1st March,
1878, and was issued with a notice that the author would not be
able for the time to continue *Fors*, as his medical advisers had
ordered absolute rest. The fourth number is dated March, 1880,
and the fifth September, 1880. Since then there have been no
further issues of *Fors*.

Fors, he explains, "is the best part of three good English
words, Force, Fortitude, and Fortune." The root of the adjective
Claviger being either, as he likes to put it, *clava*, a club; *clavis*,
a key; or, *clavus*, a nail or a rudder; and *gero* meaning to carry,
"Clavigera may mean, therefore, either club-bearer, key-bearer,
or nail-bearer. Each of these three possible meanings of
Clavigera corresponds to one of the three meanings of Fors.
Fors, the club-bearer, means the strength of Hercules, or of
Deed. Fors, the key-bearer, means the strength of Ulysses, or
of Patience. Fors, the nail-bearer, means the strength of
Lycurgus, or of Law." (*Fors*, No. ii., pp. 2–3; and cf. iii. 5,
and xv. 15.) A *Letter to Young Girls*, which appeared in *Fors*
of 1876, has gone through three or more editions as a separate
tract.

As Slade Professor Mr. Ruskin delivered seven *Lectures on Art*
before the University of Oxford in Hilary Term, 1870, and they
were printed in the same year at the Clarendon Press. After
the inaugural discourse the subjects are the relation of art to
religion, the relation of art to morals, the relation of art to
use, and the more technical subjects of line, light, and colour.
To accompany this there was printed in the same year a *Catalogue*

of Examples arranged for Study in the University Galleries. Mr.
Ruskin, again as Slade Professor, in 1870, gave lectures on the
elements of sculpture before the University of Oxford, and two
years later printed six of them under the title of *Aratra Pentelici—*
i.e., the Ploughs of Pentelicus, a mountain in Attica where marble
abounded. This contains a great deal also relating to the artistic
aspect of numismatics. One of the plates is that never-to-be-
forgotten comparison of the Apollo of Syracuse and a self-made
man of the present day glorifying his own maker. The seventh
lecture on sculpture was issued in 1872 in a separate form, and
sets forth the *Relation between Michael Angelo and Tintoretto.* It
was printed thus that it might be used at once in reference to the
drawings exhibited in the galleries, and with a warning word that its
business is to point out "what is to be blamed in Michael Angelo
and that it assumes the facts of his power to be generally known."
The *Eagle's Nest* is a collection of ten lectures on the relation of
natural science to art, which were given before the University of
Oxford in Lent Term in 1872, and printed in the same year.
Ariadne Florentina is the title given to six lectures on wood and
metal engraving, given before the University of Oxford in
Michaelmas Term of 1872. These deal with the relation of
engraving to other arts in Florence, to the technics of wood and
metal engraving, to design in the German schools of engraving as
represented by Dürer and Holbein, and in the Florentine schools
by Sandro Botticelli. There is an appendix to the volume,
which was printed in 1876, on the present state of engraving in
England. The volume entitled *Val d'Arno* contains ten lectures
on the Tuscan art directly antecedent to the Florentine year of
victories, given before the University of Oxford in Michaelmas
Term, 1873, and printed in the following year. The main subject
is the art-work of Niccolo and Giovanni Pisano. All the above-
named volumes are illustrated by plates, &c., many of them from
Ruskin's originals.

Mr. Ruskin's love of nature is shown under another phase in
the lectures on Greek and English birds given before the University of Oxford, and printed in 1873 under the title of *Love's
Meinie.* This is the old French *meiny*, a household or retinue of
servants. Only two parts have so far appeared. The first deals
with the robin, and the second with the swallow. The title

appears to have been suggested by the description in the *Romance of the Rose* of the God of Love, whose robe has on it figures of birds, whilst around him fly living birds :—

> But nightingales, a full great rout
> That flien over his head about,
> The leaves felden as they flien
> And he was all with birds wrien,
> With popinjay, with nightingale,
> With chelaundre, and with wodewale,
> With finch, with lark, and with archangel.
> He seemed as he were an angell.
> That down were comen from Heaven clear.

Proserpina began in 1875; and the parts then issued were published as vol. i. in 1879. It is still incomplete. It is, as the title-page tells us, a series of "studies of wayside flowers, while the air was yet pure among the Alps, and in the Scotland and England which my father knew." The title is chosen with reference to the lines in the *Winter's Tale*, act iv., sc. iii., ll. 116-118. In the introduction he gives advice which few of us will wish to see followed : "If any scientific man thinks his labours are worth the world's attention, let him also [like Linnæus] write what he has to say in Latin, finishedly and exquisitely, if it take him a month to do a page. But if—which, unless he be one of the chosen of millions, is assuredly the fact—his lucubrations are only of local and temporary consequence, let him write, as clearly as he can, in his native language."

One purpose of the book is to interpret for the young the Latin or Greek names, altering some of the names because they are "founded on some unclean or debasing association," so that "children who learn botany on the system adopted in this book will know the useful and beautiful names of the plants hitherto given, in all languages; the useless and ugly ones they will not know." Whilst insisting on the learning of the Latin, Mr. Ruskin would also preserve the English names, some of which mirror poetic fancies as beautiful as the flowers. This work is illustrated by some fine specimens of Mr. Ruskin's own artistic powers.

Of *Deucalion* the first part appeared in 1875, the seventh in 1880. The first six make vol. i., which was issued in 1879. The seventh part is the lecture on Snakes, delivered at the London

Institution on St. Patrick's Day. It is still incomplete. The object of the book is to present to the public "collected studies of the lapse of waves, and life of stones." In the time of Deucalion, according to the classic story, the deluge came on the earth. Mr. Ruskin's familiarity with the sciences of geology and mineralogy is well known. In the introduction to the present work he says :—

> But I think it due to my readers, that they may receive what real good there may be in these studies with franker confidence, to tell them that the first sun-portrait ever taken at the Matterhorn (and as far as I know of any Swiss mountain whatever) was taken by me in the year 1849; that the outlines (drawn by measurement of angle), given in *Modern Painters*, of the Cervin, and aiguilles of Chamouni, are at this day demonstrable by photography as the trustworthiest then in existence; that I was the first to point out, in my lecture given in the Royal Institution, the real relation of the vertical cleavages to the stratification in the limestone ranges belonging to the chalk formation in Savoy; and that my analysis of the structure of agates (*Geological Magazine*) remains, even to the present day, the only one which has the slightest claim to accuracy of distinction or completeness of arrangement.

The work contains lectures on the Alps and the Jura, the symbolic use of the colours of precious stones in heraldry, and on Yewdale and its streamlets, in addition to some controversial matter respecting glacial theories.

The *Mornings in Florence* came out in 1875, and are intended as a further performance of the "real duty" involved in his Oxford professorship, by giving "simple studies of Christian art for English travellers." The book is in the form of letters "written as I would write to any of my friends who asked me what they ought preferably to study in limited time." The first part deals with Giotto's work at Santa Croce; the second describes his painting of the meeting of Joachim and Anna at the Golden Gate in the church of Sta Maria Novella; the third part, "Before the Soldan," deals with Giotto's pictures of the life of St. Francis of Assisi, and especially of that where that noble Italian stands before "the best of Paynim chivalry to declare the message of the gospel." The fifth part, "The Vaulted Book," describes the "Spanish Chapel" of Sta Maria Novella, which is continued in the next part under the title of the "Strait Gate." The sixth part is "The Shepherd's Tower," and explains the meanings of the bas reliefs in which Giotto has given us his views of the mysteries of life and of religion. The *Mornings in Florence* have been left so far incomplete, the last belonging to the year 1876.

The *Bibliotheca Pastorum* has already been named. The series bearing that name began in 1876, and the two volumes, so far issued, are the *Economist* of Xenophon and *Rock Honeycomb*, a selection from Sir Philip Sidney's Psalter. Each of these works has a preface and notes by the editor. In 1880 appeared *Elements of English Prosody*, which was intended, we are told on the title page, for use in St. George's Schools, and is explanatory of the various terms used in *Rock Honeycomb*. In 1876 he acted as editor to the excellent volume on the *Art Schools of Mediæval Christendom* by Miss A. C. Owen.

Venice is the subject of some of his smaller works. *St. Mark's Rest* (1877) is described as the History of Venice written for the help of the few travellers who still care for his monuments. It was intended to extend to twelve parts and two supplements. Two parts only have been issued, and one supplement devoted to a description of the pictures by Carpaccio in the chapel of San Giorgio de' Schiavoni. Mr. Ruskin issued in the same year a *Guide to the principal Pictures in the Academy of the Fine Arts at Venice*, intended in a similar manner for the use of English travellers.

His views on the teaching of art are further explained and exemplified in *The Laws of Fésole*, of which vol. i. appeared in 1879, having been issued in parts during 1877-8. The title is derived from the hermit home of Angelico, and the book is "a familiar treatise on the elementary principles and practice of drawing and painting as determined by the Tuscan masters." Mr. Ruskin regards the very name of Schools of Design as involving "the profoundest of Art fallacies. Drawing may be taught by tutors but Design only by Heaven; and to every scholar who thinks to sell his inspiration Heaven refuses its help." The first chapter is headed by that pregnant sentence, "All great art is praise." Some of the aphorisms contain instruction put in a humorous form :—

"Please paint me my white cat," said little Imelda. "Child," answered the Bolognese Professor, "in the grand school all cats are grey."

Be economical in everything, but especially in candles. When it is time to light them, go to bed. But the worst waste of them is drawing by them.

"I can do what I like with my colours, now," said the proud young scholar. "So could I at your age," answered the master; "but now, I can only do what other people like."

The title is thus explained :—

Under the term "Laws of Fésole," therefore, may be most strictly and accurately arranged every principle of art, practised at its purest source, from the twelfth to the fifteenth century inclusive. And the purpose of this book is to teach our English students of art the elements of these Christian laws, as distinguished from the Infidel laws of the spuriously classic school, under which, of late, our students have been exclusively trained. Nevertheless, in this book the art of Giotto and Angelico is not taught because it is Christian, but because it is absolutely true and good; neither is the Infidel art of Palladio and Giulio Romano forbidden because it is Pagan; but because it is false and bad; and has entirely destroyed not only our English schools of art, but all others in which it has ever been taught, or trusted in.

Fésole, an eminence hard by Florence, is introduced by Milton in his great epic, with the accent on the last syllable, as one of the places whence Galileo studied the heavens (Book i., l. 289).

This book is called *The Laws of Fésole* because the entire system of possible Christian Art is founded on the principles established by Giotto in Florence, he receiving them from the Attic Greeks through Cimabue, the last of their disciples, and engrafting them on the existing art of the Etruscans, the race from which both his master and he were descended.—(Preface, pp. xii, xiii.)

He therefore ranges under the term every principle of art, practised at its purest source, from the twelfth to the fifteenth century inclusive. Plate iii. of the *Ariadne Florentina*, page 114, is a reproduction of Baccïo Bandini's Astrologia, under which is engraved Milton's line, above referred to :—

At ev'ning, from the top of Fesolè.

In March, 1878, there was an exhibition of the Turner drawings belonging to Mr. Ruskin at the Fine Art Society's Galleries. For this Mr. Ruskin issued a thin volume of explanatory *Notes*. The epilogue, left incomplete through the writer's illness, contains much interesting matter respecting his early acquisition of Turner's drawings. A very sumptuous edition of these notes, with illustrations in photogravure has also appeared. How sadly falls the sound of the words with which Mr. Ruskin closes his preface :—

Morning breaks as I write, along those Coniston Fells, and the level mists, motionless and grey beneath the rose of the moorlands, veil the lower woods, and the sleeping village, and the long lawns by the lake-shore. Oh, that some one had but told me, in my youth, when all my heart seemed to be set on these colours and clouds, that appear for a little while then vanish away, how little my love of them would serve me, when the silence of lawn and wood, in the dews of morning, should be completed ; and all my thoughts be of those whom, by neither, I was to meet more !

For the loan collection of the drawings of Samuel Prout and William Hunt, exhibited at the Fine Art Galleries in 1879–80, Mr. Ruskin printed some *Notes* which contain in a discursive form a critical estimate of those artists.

In 1880 appeared *Arrows of the Chace*, a collection of scattered letters published in the daily newspapers from 1840 to 1880. They were collected and edited by an Oxford pupil, whose name has not been made known, and were introduced by a preface of the author, who found that in the entire mass of them there was not a word he wished to change, or a statement to retract, and, he adds, " I believe few pieces of advice which the reader will not find it for his good to act upon." These two volumes contain short deliverances upon a wide variety of topics. In the first we have matters relating to art criticism and education, public institutions and the National Gallery, Pre-Raphaelitism, Turner, Architecture, and Restoration, some letters on geological topics and miscellaneous epistles on the study of natural history and other matters. The second volume deals with makers of politics and war, including the Italian question, the Jamaica Insurrection, the Franco-Prussian war, matters of political economy, and miscellaneous letters on the management of railways, servants and houses, Roman inundations, education for rich and poor, women, their work and dress ; literary criticisms, dramatic reform, and a variety of other topics.

In 1880 appeared *Our Fathers have told us*, a thin pamphlet of " Sketches of the history of Christendom for boys and girls who have been held at its fonts." This first part, " the Bible of

Amiens," deals with the story of St. Martin of Tours. The preface ends with these words :—

> It has been told them in the Laws of Fésole that all great Art is Praise. So is all faithful History and all high Philosophy. For these three, Art, History, and Philosophy, are each but one part of the Heavenly Wisdom, which seeth not as man seeth, but with Eternal Charity, and because she rejoices not in iniquity, *therefore* rejoices in the Truth.
>
> For true knowledge is of Virtue only; of poisons and vices, it is Hecate who teaches, not Athena. And of all wisdom, chiefly the Politician's must consist in this divine Prudence; it is not, indeed, always necessary for men to know the virtues of their friends or their masters; since the friend will still manifest and the master use. But woe to the Nation which is too cruel to cherish the virtue of its subjects, and too cowardly to recognize that of its enemies !"

In 1880 was published *The Lord's Prayer and the Church.* Mr. Ruskin, at the suggestion of the Rev. F. A. Malleson (vicar of Broughton-in-Furness), wrote some letters on the question, "What is a Clergyman of the Church of England?" and "Can this Gospel of Christ be put into such plain words and short terms that a plain man may understand it?" He then comments upon the Lord's Prayer clause by clause as an epitome or synopsis of Christian faith. These letters were read to the Clerical Society, of which Mr. Malleson was secretary, and also to the Brighton and Ormskirk Societies. They were first privately printed, then appeared in the *Contemporary Review,* December, 1879, and finally were gathered into a volume for the public, with the addition of essays and comments by Mr. Malleson, letters concerning them from various members of the clergy and laity, and an epilogue by Mr. Ruskin.

This lengthy list by no means represents the full extent of Mr. Ruskin's literary activity. What have been named are his principal works, but in addition he has contributed to the *Architectural Magazine, Quarterly Review,** the *Contemporary,* the *Nineteenth Century,* and other reviews, to the Transactions of the Royal Institute of British Architects, of the Geological and of the Meteorological Societies. In *Fors* (No. lxxv., Dec., 1875) he

---

* His two articles in the *Quarterly* are :—1. A review of Lord Lindsay's *History of Christian Art* (June, 1847) ; and 2, a review of Eastlake on the *History of Painting* (March, 1848).

states that he had seven books in the press at once—"and any one of them enough to take up the remainder of my life." We have his own testimony that he has also collections for other works. In the preface to *Deucalion* (1875) he says :—

> Of these materials, I have now enough by me for a more interesting (in my own opinion) history of fifteenth-century Florentine art, in six octavo volumes; an analysis of the Attic art of the fifth century B.C., in three volumes; an exhaustive history of northern thirteenth-century art, in ten volumes; a life of Turner, with analysis of modern landscape art, in four volumes; a life of Walter Scott, with analysis of epic art, in seven volumes; a life of Xenophon, with analysis of the general principles of Education, in ten volumes; a commentary on Hesiod, with final analysis of the principles of Political Economy, in nine volumes; and a general description of the geology and botany of the Alps, in twenty-four volumes.

What, then, is the teaching of Ruskin,—taught with so much passion and fervour, with such wealth of illustration, with such power and melody of language ? It is that Art should be true to Nature, and that Man should be true to God. When Art loses its faith in Nature, it ceases to possess utility. When Man ceases to work Righteousness, there follow disorders and social perils of every kind. Ruskin beholds in our modern society an aristocracy which has abdicated its functions, a middle class largely given up to greed, a working class struggling in the dark, but dimly conscious of injustice. He sees the fair fields replaced by " jerry-built " houses, the lechery, the drunkenness, the brutality that disgrace our towns and degrade men and women below the level of the beasts, and put them on a par with the fiends of the pit. He says we want Reverence, Obedience, and Organization, to grapple with these evils. He not only denounces the wrong, but has a method for its redress. Even if it prove impracticable, we still owe him a debt of gratitude. He has taught us, perhaps more than any man, the glory of the visible universe. He has taught us also that it is an ill return for God's gift of delight in beauty and order to leave our brethren festering in misery and despair.

A. Ireland & Co., Printers, Manchester.